Live an Authentic Life

The Crabapple Tree

Merry Christmas
Amari!
With love from
Great Grandma Lyn

Tom O'Toole, Jr.

What others are saying about The Crabapple Tree...

"In the many years that I have known Tom O'Toole everything he has done has been marked by an abundance of empathy, kindness and love. Thus, I can think of no one better to explore this sensitive and timely topic, especially for children. Tom infuses this sweet allegory with insights that can only come from personal experience. Drawing on his own journey, Tom has written a finely crafted story that will resonate with every child, every parent, every family that reads it. The Crabapple Tree will illuminate their path to acceptance, love and happiness."

Maureen Flatley
Child Welfare Advocate and Government Relations Strategist

"Our society has made us oppressors of ourselves; the enemy is us! Tom O'Toole's experience is not different from thousands of people all around the world yearning to breathe free. This book holds the secret kept by many to this day, and I am a firm believer Tom's experience will help not just children but also parents to understand this dynasty. We as a society need to build firm bridges for our younger generation. The time to act is now!"

Edafe Okporo
Host of The Pont Podcast
Author of Bed 26: A Memoir of an African Man's Asylum in the United States

"Tom's work captures the essence of societal ideas about 'knowers and knowing'—which albeit are made up of the dominant discourse and constructs of created norms and ideas. The Crabapple Tree knew its own truth and had the courage to remain steadfast, in spite of the voices of those who attempted to eradicate it. Bravo, Tom, for having the courage to tell this story!"

Maria Rose, LICSW
Christian Counselor

"The Crabapple Tree is an important message to children and adults and reminds me of the line in Shakespeare, 'This above all: to thine own self be true.' Lessons in early childhood have a way of shaping our lives. Children who read this book will be richer and more like 'Hopeful' and we will all be better for it."

Mossik Hacobian
Executive Director, Boston's Higher Ground

"This story melted my heart!! It is a story about finding yourself, love for family, love for things, persistence, determination, and family coming together."

Maritza Juliao
Executive Director, Crispus Attucks Children's Center

Dedication

For my family, Tom O'Toole, Sr., Shirley O'Toole, Arlene Christianson, Brenda Drolet, and my best friend, Christopher Koukos. Thank you for loving me and for teaching me how to love the differences in all of us.

In loving memory of my dear little brother, Michael O'Toole, who died when he was two and I was four. I love you, Mikey. I'll never forget you.

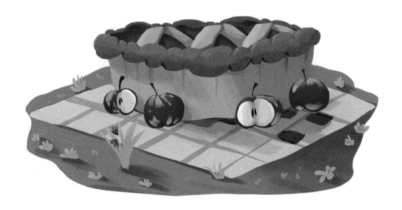

Cover Design by www.100covers.com
Interior Formatting by www.formattedbooks.com

Acknowledgments

Life is so much more interesting, fun, inspiring, and worth living when we learn to live it with each other. You would not be reading this story had it not been for the loving, caring, candid, and sometimes brutally honest support of the following individuals: Jeff Bass, Arlene Christianson, Joanne Dolan, Brenda Drolet, Paul Fallon, Devin Ferreira, Christian Grenier, Tom Griffith, Jed Jurchenko (Coach Jed the Jedi Coach), Christopher Koukos, Jesse Lewis, Elijah Mickelson, Natalene Ong, Dana Wade, and my Editor Extraordinaire, Melissa Wuske.

I would also like to acknowledge the steadfast love of my community of faith at River of Life Church in the Jamaica Plain neighborhood of Boston. We have walked together for many years exploring how a guy like me can integrate faith with sexuality at a church like yours. Not all of us agree on everything, but we are committed to loving each other as we learn to follow the leading of the Greatest Voice in everything we do. Peace and love to each of you!

Introduction

The Crabapple Tree is about bravery, courage, and standing up in the face of seemingly insurmountable opposition, criticism, judgment, and invalidation of personal identity. It is about crushed hope that is restored and dreams that were snuffed out being rekindled. It is about the gender-neutral artist who was told over and over again, "You will never amount to anything if you follow your creative heart." It is about the athletic girl who was told, "You aren't pretty enough," or the sensitive boy who was told, "Real men don't cry." It is about the non-traditional family with two moms or two dads who are told, "Your union is dishonorable, and you are a threat to my religious liberty." And it is about me, a gay boy who grew up in a whirlwind of pious legalism, convinced that something was terribly wrong with me. It is a story of hope deferred and a renewed belief in the fulfillment of longing. It is a story that elevates the marginalized and calls forth the ostracized. It is a story about the Greatest Voice speaking into the hopeless heart saying, "I see you. I made you. I love you. I want you. Never forget that love is love is love."

The Crabapple Tree

12/7/20

Amari,

Always listen for
the Greatest Voice!

Tom O'Toole, Jr.

12/1/20

Amari,

Always listen for
the Greatest Voice!

Tom B'riabery

*S*ome time ago when most grownups thought they knew everything about trees, there was a little boy whose name was Hopeful. He was part of a family and there were five of them: a daddy, a mommy, a little girl, her little brother, and a baby girl. But at that time they were a sad family who was trying to forget something. You see, there were five of them, but there should have been six of them. One other little boy had died, and so they were sad.

The family was on a quest. They were searching for a new house to live in. They dreamed about living in a house someplace away from the busy city and away from the painful memories of the little boy who had died. And so they searched everywhere for a new house. They looked at this house and said, "This one isn't just right. Too big." And they looked at that house and said, "Nope. That one isn't perfect. Too small." They searched and searched and searched, looking at house after house after house. And then one day they finally found their dream house. And the daddy and mommy said, "This is the perfect house for our family! This will become our home." The sad family was not so sad anymore.

"An apple tree! Wow!"

They moved into their new dream home, and they all went out into the backyard to have a look around. In the center of the yard there stood a strong, young tree, but it was late in the autumn, just before winter, so the tree was bare. Hopeful said, "I like that tree. It looks like a good tree. What kind of tree is that?"

The daddy looked and pondered. "I'm not completely sure, but I think that's an apple tree. It's almost winter, so we'll have to wait until spring to see for sure."

"An apple tree! Wow!" Hopeful exclaimed. He looked at the good tree in wonder and imagined what kind of apples it might grow. "I can't wait to see what kind of apples it will give us! Will they be big and red, or big and yellow, or big and green? I don't care. I just love apples, because an apple is an apple is an apple!" said the boy.

3

—*he didn't care, because an apple is an apple is an apple.*

4

Sometimes Hopeful would go out into the yard and look at the good tree, exploring it and imagining its coming transformation in the spring.

Then winter came with its wind and its snow and its ice. Hopeful would look out the window at the good tree, covered in snow and ice, and he would dream of apples, big and red, big and yellow, big and green—he didn't care, because an apple is an apple is an apple.

Hopeful's heart raced when he first saw the buds.

6

Spring arrived, and the snow melted, and the ice melted, and tiny buds began to form on the good tree. Hopeful's heart raced when he first saw the buds. He ran home from school every day to watch the buds turn to leaves, and the leaves grew and grew and grew until the tree became full and beautiful. The daddy looked at the tree and said, "Yup! Just as I suspected. This is an apple tree." Hopeful was overwhelmed with joy!

7

In the miracle of spring, blossoms formed on the good tree.

April showers brought May flowers, and in the miracle of spring, blossoms formed on the good tree. And as spring waned and the heat of summer arrived, the blossoms fell to the ground, leaving tiny little orbs in their place. "Apples! Apples! Apples!" exclaimed Hopeful. "Will they be big and red, or big and yellow, or big and green? I don't care, because an apple is an apple is an apple."

"Red! Yellow! Green! Big, juicy,
reddish-yellowish-greenish apples! Wahoo!"

Summer progressed with its warm showers and its hot rays of sunshine, and the orbs grew. Then the apples began to show color, and the boy was amazed to see that his apples were reddish-yellowish-greenish, as if they could not decide what color to be and so they chose to be all the colors. Hopeful shouted one day from the yard, "Red! Yellow! Green! Big, juicy, reddish-yellow-ish-greenish apples! Wahoo!" But as summer began to fade, it became clear that these apples were different. They were not getting big, they stayed smaller than usual apples.

Early in the autumn, Hopeful picked an apple and ate it, and it was juicy, tart, and delicious. They were not big apples; they were small apples. He didn't care, be-cause an apple is an apple is an apple.

"Why do you keep that tree in your yard? That's a bad tree.
It doesn't grow real apples," said Educated.

Later in the autumn, some Vexing Voices, who caused worry and trouble, named Educated and Snooty came to the home to speak with the daddy and mommy. They thought they were smarter and better than everyone.

"Why do you keep that tree in your yard? That's a bad tree. It doesn't grow real apples," said Educated.

Snooty said, "That's a Crabapple Tree. You need to cut it down and replace it with a tree that will give you the kind of fruit that you want. You don't want those apples. They're not real."

The daddy and the mommy believed Educated and Snooty, and they decided they needed to get rid of the Crabapple Tree and replace it with a real apple tree.

13

"That Crabapple Tree doesn't give us real apples. We need to get rid of it and replace it, so we can get real apples."

14

One day late in the autumn, just before winter, Hopeful came home from school and his daddy and mommy said, "We're sorry, son, but our apple tree is bad. We need to cut it down and replace it with a real apple tree. That Crabapple Tree doesn't give us real apples. We need to get rid of it and replace it, so we can get real apples."

Hopeful was very sad, but he trusted his daddy and mommy. The Vexing Voices, Educated and Snooty, came back with some of their friends, Well-Meaning, who tried but usually failed to do what's right, and Condescending, who looked down on people they thought were worse than them. They all went out in the backyard with the daddy and the mommy. Hopeful was afraid, but he joined them because he trusted them. They all had saws and axes that the Vexing Voices brought. Even Hopeful was given his own little ax to chop with. They sawed and chopped and cut and hacked until that tree fell down leaving behind only a stump and some roots in the ground. Hopeful cried.

Hopeful began to lose some of his hope.

16

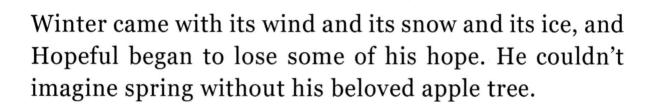

Winter came with its wind and its snow and its ice, and Hopeful began to lose some of his hope. He couldn't imagine spring without his beloved apple tree.

"Get rid of that tree! Cut it down! Cut it down! Cut it down!"

Then came spring, and before daddy and mommy had a chance to plant a new tree, a miracle happened. The Crabapple Tree reappeared, a little bit bigger and a little bit stronger than it had been when it was cut down. Hopeful was stunned and confused. That summer the same, small, reddish-yellowish-greenish, juicy, tart, delicious apples grew, and Hopeful ate them and loved them. But the Vexing Voices came back with more of their friends.

"That's a very bad tree. Those are not real apples!" yelled Educated and Snooty.

"You need to cut that tree down and replace it with a real apple tree!" shouted Well-Meaning and Condescending.

"You don't want that kind of fruit! It's not sweet enough!" bellowed Religious, who really believed that he was speaking the truth, and his friend Shaming, who always managed to make everyone believe lies about themselves.

Then, all together the Vexing Voices shouted, "Get rid of that tree! Cut it down! Cut it down! Cut it down!"

They sawed and chopped and cut and hacked...

20

Again, late in the autumn, just before winter, the Vexing Voices went out into the yard with the daddy, mommy and Hopeful. They sawed and chopped and cut and hacked until that tree fell down leaving behind only a stump and some roots in the ground. Hopeful wept.

Winter came again with its wind and its snow and its ice. And the hope that Hopeful had was becoming buried beneath the frost.

Spring returned, and the miracle happened again.

Spring returned, and the miracle happened again. The good tree came back from the dead, and it was even bigger and stronger than it had been the previous year. And those small, beautiful, reddish-yellowish-green-ish, juicy, tart apples grew. More of them! And Hopeful couldn't help but notice how they resembled and joined with the growing collection of fall foliage colors that surrounded them. In the early autumn, Hopeful picked the apples and ate them, and he loved them. In fact, he made Crabapple pie, Crabapple muffins, and Crabapple sauce to share with his family and friends.

Hopeful's worthlessness deepened,
and his hope began to turn to bitterness.

24

The Vexing Voices returned and shouted boldly, "This bad tree can't be allowed to stay in your yard. We must cut it down and rip it out by the roots!" So late in the autumn, just before winter, everyone went out into the yard, and they sawed and chopped and cut and hacked until that tree fell down. This time they ripped out the stump by the roots, and they burned the tree and the stump and the roots, leaving a big, empty hole in the ground. Hopeful sobbed, but he tried to trust in the people he loved.

Winter came again with its wind and its ice and its snow. Hopeful's worthlessness deepened, and his hope began to turn to bitterness. It was so hard to imagine life without his precious tree. He dreamed of spring days when he would sit under the good tree and watch the birds flitting in and out of its graceful branches. He closed his eyes and tried to imagine how his Crabapple Tree provided shade from the hot summer sun as he laid in the grass beneath its canopy. He could almost hear the crunch of the first bite of the first apple he ate every autumn, and he could almost smell the tart, sticky juice that sometimes dripped from his lips and splashed onto his hand.

25

Miraculously in the spring, that Crabapple Tree reappeared,
even stronger, even bigger than it had ever been.

Miraculously in the spring, that Crabapple Tree reappeared, even stronger, even bigger than it had ever been. But the Vexing Voices came again and again and again, and for twenty-five years, they all tried to get rid of that good tree by sawing and chopping and cutting and hacking, but every spring, that good tree reappeared, and it grew stronger and bigger and it produced more and more beautiful, little, reddish-yellowish-greenish, juicy, tart apples every summer. Hopeful picked the apples and ate them, and he loved them.

So Hopeful determined in his heart that day
that he would no longer try to get rid of his good tree.

After twenty-five years Hopeful was no longer a little boy—he had become a man. Late in the autumn, just before winter, days before the scheduled annual killing of his cherished Crabapple Tree, Hopeful went out into the yard and he looked at the good tree with tears in his eyes. "I love you, Crabapple Tree," he said. "I love your apples. They are not big and red, or big and yellow, or big and green. They are small, reddish-yellow-ish-greenish apples, but I don't care, because an apple is an apple is an apple." So Hopeful determined in his heart that day that he would no longer try to get rid of his good tree. He would let his love for the tree grow, and he would tell the people in his life to stop trying to kill his good Crabapple Tree.

*The good Crabapple Tree survived that year,
standing strong to this very day.*

When the Vexing Voices came to murder his tree again, Hopeful stood boldly in front of that good tree and said, "This is a real apple tree. It gives me real apples. They might not be big and red, or big and yellow, or big and green. They are beautiful, small, reddish-yellowish-greenish, juicy, tart delicious Crabapples. They are real apples. An apple is an apple is an apple. Leave my tree alone!" One by one, the Vexing Voices left with their saws and their axes, and the good Crabapple Tree survived that year, standing strong to this very day.

"I made this good tree. I love this Crabapple Tree. I gave this good Crabapple Tree to you. It gives you real apples, son. An apple is an apple is an apple."

Many years have come and gone since that day, and Hopeful's love for his Crabapple Tree is rising. His daddy, mommy, and two sisters love it when Hopeful brings them Crabapple pie, Crabapple muffins, and Crabapple sauce. Hopeful knows in his heart that his little brother who died is looking down from Heaven at the good Crabapple Tree and loves it just as much as Hopeful does. The friends Hopeful cares about are also learning to love his Crabapple Tree. Not all of them. Some Vexing Voices still say or think to themselves, "Cut it down! Cut it down! Cut it down!"

But Hopeful is learning not to listen to them. His heart is growing stronger and his sadness and bitterness are fading away because instead of listening to the Vexing Voices, he is listening to the Greatest Voice, who tells Hopeful every day, "I made this good tree. I love this Crabapple Tree. I gave this good Crabapple Tree to you. It gives you real apples, son. An apple is an apple is an apple."

Tommy O'Toole, Jr. 1967
Billerica, Massachusetts
In the backyard of the "dream home" that inspired
the story of the Crabapple Tree

- Free coloring pages.
- Free conversation starter questions for parents and caregivers.
- Enter your email at www.tomotoole.net to receive your free Crabapple Tree gifts today!

46810349R00024